REFLECTIONS

REFLECTIONS

Poetry, Essays, Flash Fiction, and Short Stories

Lorraine Martin Bennett

BOOKLOGIX®

Alpharetta, Georgia

ISBN: 978-1-6653-1089-5 - Paperback
eISBN: 978-1-6653-1090-1 - eBook

Library of Congress Control Number: 2025918763

⊗This paper meets the requirements of ANSI/NISO Z39.48-1992 (Permanence of Paper)

The cover image and photographs in this book were taken by the author with the exception of Nike of Samothrace and Tiananmen Square.

0 9 2 2 2 5

This book is dedicated to the high school English and journalism teachers who first told me I might have a gift for writing, to the family members who encouraged me to develop that gift, to the wonderful friends at N.C. Writers' Network West who listened to my poetry and prose, and to BookLogix for making it happen.

Contents

FLASH FICTION, ESSAYS, AND SHORT STORIES

POEMS

Little Things

The world spins fast around me
While I stand all alone.
As I turn and look about me
I see how time has flown.

I feel so unimportant,
As useless as the breeze
That trips along its merry way,
Whispering through the trees.

But if a tiny ripple
Is all that I should be,
Then let me be a ripple
Upon a mighty sea.

And if a tiny piece of earth
Is all I'm to possess,
Let me be a mountain
With white clouds on my crest.

If I'm to be a blade of grass
Among clover blossoms white,
Let me stand both straight and proud,
And make a meadow bright.

If I'm to be a drop of dew
Upon a budding rose,
Then let me glow with diamond's hue
As the sunlight comes and goes.

For the world would be so bleak, so bare,
Without these little things.
They're the stuff of inspiration,
The gifts that all life brings.

Published in the Cherokee Scout, *Murphy, North Carolina, 1962*

The Whippoorwill

In the whispering twilight
A whippoorwill's plaintive call laments,
Breaking the stillness of oncoming night.

The somber, shallow echo rings
Above myriads of murmuring voices;
Bereaved, anxious sounds the twilight brings.

Again, his melancholy cry
Between the interim of two sleeps
Calls the silent stranger to fly,
Fly, fly away
From the glaring, coverless light of day.

1963

Parting

Ironic: as the ebbing web of time
Spins out its futile thread,
Elusive, clinging thoughts entwine
Darkened, silent souls in words unsaid.
Rhapsody in Blue haunts trembling minds
That cannot grasp "Farewell, farewell."
Raindrops drip reluctant, tired designs,
Weaving an enigmatic spell
Upon a window glass whose pane is broken,
Shattered by the fervent words unspoken.

Written during student days at Brevard College, 1963

Alone at Dusk

As empty dusk parades her sullen stars
Arrayed in murky robes of clutching night,
Loneliness pervades the searching heart
Loosing tears that blind dark eyes from light.

A solitary shadow lost in black,
A face uplifted into misty rain,
A twisted heart to crushed to cry aloud,
A being cursed to never laugh again

Walks slowly down a silent, sand-drenched shore
Unmindful of the tantalizing sea;
Lost in dreams too far away to reach,
In search of rainbows that can never be.

1963

A Shadow on Time

Glittering sands and pebble rocks
Halt wandering breakers teasing rocky inlets.
Sand burrowers suck life from shore and
disappear.

Rays and pulsing riptides lure careless
Adventuresome to forever sleep.
Winds sting cheeks and lips, salty gusts force
tears.

Alone
Adrift with the wind,
Attuned to the sea,
Shifts and shapes, its destiny
No bounds confining or defining
Times to explore or dreams to defend.

So simple it is!
A shadow on time, reflected on sand.
No tomorrow, no yesterday.

The shifting rock, the eonless sea!
And me.
Now.

1974

To Pop

They told me this morning you were gone,
That He had quietly called your soul away,
Now we are left to walk the road alone
Without your friendly voice to cheer the way.
When friends like you can be with us no more,
When the strength of life has ebbed and lost its
force,
A sighing breath slips through a closing door
Leaving only memories and remorse.
When time has borne the wretched hours away,
When the warm, free tears of grief and pain have
gone,
We'll think of you and bow our heads to pray
As silent, reverent memories linger on.

Published in the Brevard College campus newspaper, the
Clarion, *in memory of a friend, 1963*

The Cambodians

While a people died, I did nothing.
I read of their agony, detached, from a distance,
I saw their mottled death-knell faces on magazine covers,
Viewed with separate horror their wizened, starving children.
I felt their hopelessness,
Twisted their pain in my mind,
But I did nothing.

I was a writer of the passing saga,
Concerned about them, more concerned about me,
My career, my golden future, my wandering spirit
Finally finding fulfillment within my own limits.
Yet those who chronicle the passing saga
Must be poised best of all
To influence, to change, to attract attention
To mass, agonizing death.
But I did nothing.

I slept at night.
I was not hungry, cold, or in fear.
My bed was warm, my sheets clean, my lover
near.
So when I felt their cries,
Saw the concern of their brothers,
Heard their words of despair,
I was not unmoved
But not moved enough.
I cared, wished I could help
But I did nothing.

1980

Tiananmen

No blood spilled here, the general said,
As if words could wash away
Visions of bleeding bodies
And twisted wreckage on
The Avenue of Eternal Peace.

They had moved
The burned-out buses,
The flattened tents,
The broken bicycles.

But voices,
Silenced by guns,
Still echo across the pavement
And from street to street.

Alone, a man stands
Facing a column
Of approaching tanks.
After photographic immortality
He is led away
To likely death
Or certain isolation
In a prison cell

Where
Like so many others,
He must cry out,
"My country, right or wrong?
"How long?
"How long?"

Written while working as a copy editor in Atlanta and watching a news crew in China pulled off the air by government officials during the broadcast of Tiananmen Square uprising, 1989.

The Rose

I rest my head near a rose.
Its petals, opulent in their camouflage
Of painful thorns beneath,
Draw me into breathy embrace
With reminiscences of debutants,
Weddings, and funerals.

Its fragrance devours me
And I no longer care
If I saw blood left on a sturdy
Mr. Lincoln thorn
Or perfect stem of
Georgia Princess
When I cut its life away.

For as it enshrouds me
I forget how its unblemished beauty
Hides the crushed ribbon,
The broken vase,
Or the polished wood
Of the coffin beneath.

2013

Christmas

It's here.
Lights, camera, action.
Lovely lights.
Too many cameras.
Too much action.
No time at all
For peaceful moments,
Appreciative thoughts,
Or why we celebrate
This holiday at all.
There's a cantata to sing,
Cards to address,
Gifts to wrap and send,
Rooms to decorate.
It never ends.
Be still and know.
The words echo
Behind our thoughts.
The small voice
Resonates

Behind our dreams.
Remember why.
Just remember.

2015

Green Leaves

Green leaves dance
In the force of the wind,
Nourished by sunlight,
Soothed by moonlight.
In the breath of a storm
Branches bend,
Flinging leaves into
Tempestuous night.

A dull dawn breaks
On a wintry sky.
Trees cringe, tattered,
Their leaves scattered.
The forest shivers
And whispers a sigh
Of dreams broken,
Of hopes shattered.

When a Child Cries

The blue Pacific
Wraps satin fingers
Around the coastline
And bounces
Slivers of sunlight
Into the sterile room.

You lie,
Tubes in your chest,
Oblivious to bright sails
And silvery laughter
Slipping by
On the April breeze.

Is a cosmic hand
Spinning life from dust
Across the universe?
Is life just a tumble
Of cracked dreams
And broken promises?

Does God hear
When a child cries?

Your Smile

Fierce as sunlight, soft as starlight
Your brightness swept my life.
Your lively dance and joyful song
Made music of mundane days.

And now that sadness
Is lifting its grip
A life and its gifts
Slip into perspective.

Its years and hours
Were not a tragedy
Though they were brief,
Choked off too soon.

For in Spring air
Throbbing with celebration
I find an outline
Hanging in my memory.

Not a sad or sunken shadow
Lined with puzzlement or pain,
Fierce as sunlight, soft as starlight,
It is your smile.

When a Child Cries *and* Your Smile *were written after the loss of a close friend.*

Passages

With apologies to Jenny Joseph, Samantha Reynolds, Dylan Thomas, and Thanatopsis

When years have passed through me
(I will not call it growing old,
For that would admit defeat)
I shall sleep when I want,
Wake when I want,
Say what I want
And what I like, I will eat.

I will swear at the telly,
Spill marmalade jelly
And opine how the world
Is going to pot
When, in reality,
How should I know
Whether it is
Or whether it's not.

And if by chance
I should make a new friend,
I will take her to dinner,
And talk of life's dance.

I will think she's a gift
And the dinner's a winner.

If she lasts through the week
I shall treasure our time
Because so many others
That I have befriended
Have drifted away
Like autumn leaves fall
When green time has ended.

I will not go gentle
Into that good night,
But rather greet sleep
As a familiar old friend.
If it comes in the night
And takes me away,
It will not be unwelcome
If it closes my eyes
And eases my end.

2018

Ode to Mac

The house is too quiet, the yard far too empty.

The rip in my heart seems to bleed on and on.

I see your brown eyes, hear your collar jangle,

Our home's not a refuge since you have been
gone.

Our cats scour the corners, they yearn for your
sounds,

The click of your large paws while you made
your rounds.

They shadow the rooms, search out every floor.

They check on the sofa, keep watch by the door.

I made you a promise your passing would come

When illness overtook you and no more could be
done.

I know how you loved me, my forever friend.

I could not watch you suffer and so made an end.

Through the eyes of my memory, you lope through the farm,

Your spaniel ears flying, coat gold in the sun.

You bound up the hills, track where deer graze,

Patrol the fence boundary your favorite ways.

There won't be another like you in my life.

My sorrow will ease, though it cuts like a knife.

I talk to your ashes, it's hardly the same.

My tears overwhelm me when I call your name.

You will live in my heart where love cords will bind

A dog and his mistress, two souls of one mind.

I'll always remember our walks in the grass.

The grief of your passing will leave me at last.

I'll treasure your memory, I'll know you're at peace.

My sadness will go and my aching will cease.

Then I'll see you running with joy in the sun,

Your spaniel ears flying, a dog having fun.

Mac, the golden cocker,
lived on the Martin Farm
August 15, 2006 –March 25, 2019

This poem was Gold Medal Winner
in Clay and Cherokee County Senior Games
Silver Arts Competition, 2020.

Our Song

The road unwinds before me,
Its ending I can't see.
Where two of us together went
Now there is only me.

We seemed to move in tandem,
Two hearts enjoined as one.
Then you went on ahead of me
And left me so alone.

We came to that sad parting.
We had to say goodbye.
Now I must keep our flame alive.
I promised I would try.

Still I'm adrift remembering.
My heart just wants to weep.
Grief and sorrow bear me down
And stalk me when I sleep.

Yet your warm smile sustains me.
I know how much you cared—
Your words, our dreams, our moments,
Those treasures we two shared.

Like the kiss of sunlight
Your memory prods me on.
Your soul now lives inside me
With our history, and our song.

March 20, 2021

*Written in Atlanta three months after I lost my
husband on Dec. 28, 2020.*

*Cherokee-Clay County Senior Games
Silver Arts Competition
First Place Gold Medal
Winner in Poetry, May 2021*

The Mountains within Me

They've always been there
Like a sigh or a teardrop.
But I failed to notice,
Or took them for granted.
As everyone knows
The familiar surrounds us,
Like breathing and rain,
And silent as prayers.

Sometimes I'm reminded
Of a steadfast endurance,
The rocks of our lives
Unmoving and solid.
Our storied Appalachians
Stretch toward the sky.
Clouds kiss their crowns,
Mists hang from their pines.

Through Clingmans Dome, Talking Rock,
Chunky Gal, Brasstown Bald,
Winds whisper and whine,
Breezes echo and beckon.
Hawks spiral and swoop,
Bears prowl, coyotes howl.

The mountains' wild creatures
Leave footfalls like raindrops.

Serene and majestic,
With weathered old shapes,
They bookend our lives
And ground our foundations.
Their tops round and beaten
By time, wind, and water
Seem unchanged to us
Yet renew with each season.

When our own lives
Are stormed and upended
By anguish and loss,
Cheered by laughter and love,
The mountains remain
To soothe and revive us,
Imparting their strengths
To share them with us.

They green with spring rains,
Flame with fall colors,
Shift with cloud covers,
Dance in the moonlight.
They give us their peace
And steady our days.

Their shapes touch our souls
And anchor our lives.

April 2021

Here to Remind Us

A whippoorwill's trill,
Violets in spring,
Butterflies at morning,
Soft midday breezes.
And in distant vistas
The far blue mountains
Whisper their greetings
And sing us their songs.

Hummingbirds come
To brighten our day,
At dusk, fireflies rise
To dance on our lawn.
Crickets at nightfall
Sing us to sleep.
Birds nest in our hedges
And wake us at dawn.

All of God's creatures
Are here to remind us
Of what we have lost
And what we have learned.
They bring us their blessings
Like soft summer rain,

We treasure these visits
Again and again.

A doe with twin fawns
Grazes the pasture.
Cottontails bounce
In tumbleweed dances.
Flowers in profusion
Unfold their colors,
Blinking like stardust
In cerulean skies.

Martins Creek sings,
Laurel Creek chuckles.
Fires Creek laughs
As it flies over rocks.
The storied Hiawassee
Churns on its way
Carrying the promise
Of sunshine today.

August 2021

Soul Wounds

Ashes.
They drift and swirl
In air and water,
Their minute footprints
Carry reminders
Of fractured relationships,
Unmet wishes.

Set fire to hateful letters.
Let forgiveness wash away
The barbs that sting,
The acts that crush,
That serve to remind
How those you love
Can hurt your heart
And wound your soul.

Time eases pain?
What an old adage.
How much time?
How many tears?
How many nights

Of waiting
For hurt to stop
Or simply subside.

Soul wounds—
They take a long time
To heal.

August 2021

Grief

Grief is a spider.
It weaves a tattered web
Over my dreams, my thoughts,
My life, my breath.
It swells in darkness,
Swings in silence.
But sometimes sunshine bursts through
And grief becomes a leaping fawn,
A singing robin, a laughing brook
Murmuring through my day.

Published in Poem, Huntsville Literary Association,
Huntsville, Alabama, 2022

Awakening

I am in Granddad's front yard,
Filled with fireflies.
Sycamore leaves carpet the ground,
The smell of decay and rebirth.
As children, we played
Chasing insects' flickering lights.
In reality, we were chasing dreams.
As adults, we would remember
A time precious, religious,
As visceral as a hand's touch.
A time long ago, yet not so long.
As alive in memory
As yesterday's
Awakening.

2022

Hope

Is it an elephant in the room?
A flyspeck on the wall?
Do I give it legs to walk
Or breath to draw
Or wings to take flight?
Is it an ocean
Or a river
Or just a rivulet among rocks?
Does it shift and change
As it weaves a path
Through my hours and days?
Or is it an ever-elusive want,
Something desired but never gained?
A reach exceeding grasp?
How I wish it will be a butterfly
Riding a summer breeze
On velvet wings!

Listening

When I am deeply listened to
I am a river
That flows between jagged rocks
But is not impeded.

When I am deeply listened to
I am the sky,
Without clouds
To interfere or sunsets to distract.

When I am deeply listened to
I am a starry night,
Serene and soft,
Without a distant thunder
To shake the silence.

When I am not listened to
I feel ignored and misunderstood,
Misused and mistaken,
And finally, mad.

When I deeply listen to someone
I take myself out of the way,
Watch their mouth,
With my ears and eyes,

And try not to focus
On how I will reply.

When I don't listen to someone
I don't recognize the worth
Of that person's wholeness.
I may have somewhere else to be.
I may be late for my next task.
I may have a distressing distraction,
Or I may not even like them.

But they might have a message
Especially for me,
An insight, a revelation,
An answer to unspoken prayer,
And if I don't listen
I will miss it.

Poems Awakening, Hope, and Listening *were written
during a poetry class in response to a prompt, 2023.*

Armless Wonder (Nike of Samothrace)

She stands atop marble stairs,
Wishing she had arms to stretch
As if to embrace the world
If she could have
But she could not
Because she has none.

She might have encircled
A lover, a friend,
A child, a sister
If she could have
But she could not
Because she has none.

She has wondrous wings
As if she could fly,
But she stands rooted
In marble solitude
At history's designation
Because she has none.

She is Nike the goddess
Trapped in her space.
This headless angel

Longs to embrace
But she could not
Because she has none.

So armless she waits,
A Samothrace Victory
With wings to fly
But no arms to hug
And no eyes to see
Because she has none.

2023

Autumn Symphony

Red maples trumpet their glorious song.
Yellow poplars join the duet
As leaves scudding across pavement
Provide percussive accompaniment.

Beech and bitternut hickory
Drop nuts, drumming the forest floor.
Slippery elm and American holly
Dance to their own polka.

Black tupelo's scarlet tune
Warbles among lofty walnuts.
Hickory and red oak blend
With sycamore's violin libretto.

Mother Nature's autumn chorus
Rolls across the Appalachians,
Its mystical music
A seasonal symphony

2023

Walking through Rain

It comes whispering,
Stroking the grass
Pattering rooftops
Clamoring across tin,
Disrupting dragonflies,
Chasing birds beneath branches,
Rabbits to warrens.

It falls slowly, then harder,
Freshens and taunts,
Rouses, awakens
My doubts, my questions,
My yearning, and finally
My hunger inside.

That's when I ponder:
Can rain cleanse my mind,
Wash away my grief,
Succor my senses,
Remove my pain,
Stoke my resolve,
Fire my ambition?

It plasters my hair,
Tracks my cheeks' tears,
Touches my tongue,
Chills my bare arms,
Puts me to wonder
When rain comes again
Will lightning and thunder
Join in the dance

Or is it
Only rain?

2024

Raven

She was light and air and water,
The very elements of life.
Her smile evoked
Grace and a caring heart.
Her dark eyes reflected
A passion for friends with
Four legs and for Mother Earth.
Her lust for life and questing mind
Revealed a spirit unbowed
By the slings and arrows
Life unleashed in her final year.
Her written words and phrases
Unmasked the heart of a poet
And the soul of a seer.
Does she sail among stars?
Does she ride on the wind?
Does she fly with the angels?
Her spirit still glows,
An unfinished symphony.

How I wish
She could have stayed longer.

March 2024

Written in honor of fellow writer and poet Raven Chiong,
1964–2023

On Loss and Gain

The empty ache of loss again.
Lover, parent, pet, or friend.
Is love a wheel of joy and pain,
Of having, losing in the end?
What does it teach, an old refrain?
What is it that we can gain?

Does loss hide another side,
That love's an ocean roiled and wide?
What lessons might it hide below?
Is there force we cannot know?
Can truth be just beyond our reach?
Or is the gap too far to breach?

If something comes each passing year
Can't it be strength as well as fear?
Is something there to help us see
A gentler, rare humanity?
Is there a peace we can attain
If truly, finally, loss is gain?

2024

Black Moon Rising

When the black moon
Marched across the face
Of our celestial neighbor,
Source of light and brightness,
We gasped, we cheered,
We cried and partied.
We danced to The Age of Aquarius,
Hummed the Theme from *2001*,
Sang along with Bonnie Tyler's
"Total Eclipse of the Heart."

600 exchanged vows in Arizona.
Thousands jammed a speedway
In Indianapolis.
Dozens traveled hours for
A ringside seat to
The cosmic spectacle.

How odd we should
Go to such extremes
For a natural phenomenon
When we never cheer and dance
In similar fashion
For tornadoes and typhoons,

Earthquakes and hurricanes
(Although sometimes we cry).

What is it
That made us pause,
Hush our complaints,
Forget our prejudices,
Put aside our rancor
And look up
Together in wonder,
United and humbled,
If for only four minutes
And touch the skies
With our eyes?

Written following the lunar eclipse, April 2024

When Words Won't Come

When words won't come
An empty page taunts,
Telling me to focus
And concentrate.

But how?
When sun is beaming,
Birds are wheeling,
Grass is growing
And flowers need water.

Who has time
To put pen to paper
Or type addled words
On a blank page
When summer is waning
And if I don't get outside soon
These long, languid days
Will turn to lengthy nights
That seem to never end?

Then maybe words
That won't come now
Will surface and flow
In brilliant sequence.

2024

Questions without Answers

Reflections on Christian Wiman's My Bright Abyss

It captivates you, draws you in,
Repels and confounds you.
You think you know
What he might mean
But you're left nevertheless
Wondering why,
And why bother at all
If the answers do not
So easily or ever come.

But the questions
Persist without answers,
Some things hidden
In places too deep,
Far too confounding
For minds to unravel.
And so you plod along,
And continue to fret over
Questions without answers.

Sometimes thinking
Perhaps that's the way
It was intended.

2024

This Day

What shall I do
With this day?

Shall I wrap it
In a box
And share it
With a friend?

Shall I put
Brush to canvas
And try
To make it stay?

Shall I craft
Words on paper
To keep what
It might tell me?

Or shall I do
None of these?

Perhaps I shall
Take a walk instead
And feel the sun
Wash over me
Like liquid dreams.

Or savor the touch
Of gentle rain
On my face and hands
And listen to birdsong,
A symphony of spring.

2025

Beginnings

Alone
Being without
Lonely
A state of place
Solitude
A learning to live
Within and without.
A time to cut strings
Of past lives,
Branch out,
Take a different road
One heavily traveled
Or traveled not at all.

Where am I
On this passage,
This self-experience?
Is awareness a key
To opening new doors
Or has it all happened
Before I can remember?

Is being alone a new adventure
Or has it always been
A shadow with my footsteps?
Is lonely a state of mind,
A place of rest,
Or a passing phase
Slipping moment to moment
Until a happy thought
Pushes it aside?
And solitude,
Is it a self-seclusion,
Much needed
To recharge the senses,
To keep the ship of self afloat
Toward far horizons?

2025

Flash Fiction, Essays, and Short Stories

The Gift

The small plane spiraled out of the sky and blasted through a row of palm trees near the street behind Pat Steven's cottage. The nightmare unfolded as she was having one of her own—riding a heaving deck, bracing against slippery planks.

She awoke to a flash, no ocean, no rocking boat, just a dresser, a chair beside her bed, proof she was conscious. The throbbing glow outside was real. She struggled into her robe and opened her front door. The usual muggy South Miami night was filled with acrid smoke.

In the street, the air was so thick she could hardly see. Someone was crying. Pat turned toward the sobs. "Come here, sweetheart. Come to me." Her own voice seemed to originate from outside her body. *I'm not dreaming,* she thought.

A toddler, pink dress blackened, eyes wild with fear, was crawling from underneath a charred bush.

Pat gathered the shivering child, feeling warmth through her robe. She smelled smoke and fuel in the little girl's hair.

A firetruck careened by, followed by two police cars. Someone shouted, "Here's one. She's alive!" A burly uniformed man reached for the child, who reinforced her hold on Pat's neck and would not let go.

"Ma'am, do you know this child?" The uniformed man's tone was sharp. "Is she injured?"

"She doesn't seem to be. She came from under that bush," Pat heard her own voice again. *I must be awake in the middle of this madness*, she thought. She was aware the man was staring at her.

The officer pried the child's arms from Pat's neck and handed her to ambulance attendants. Red emergency lights flared as the vehicle disappeared down the street. Pat could still hear sobs on her shoulder, see fear-filled eyes. A familiar feeling washed over her. Brushing away tears, she turned toward her cottage.

A few hours later, her bungalow seemed too quiet after last night's chaos. Many Saturdays began this way, over coffee and newspapers, since Charlie died. Weekend mornings, their special togetherness time to play and plan, were hardest to endure. They were two dreamers with schooling behind, shining futures ahead. Charlie had opened his law practice. She had nailed a coveted job with the city's largest accounting firm.

They celebrated with a new sedan for her, sailboat for him. The sudden appearance of two friends at the front door had changed everything, including the shape of her dreams. An unexpected squall and a sailboat shattered on rocks left her with nightmares of capsized boats. A vacant space at the breakfast table greeted her mornings.

She read the newspaper's recap of last night's events: a twelve-seat commuter plane, ten bodies recovered, one survivor, a girl, about two, bruised, unidentified, and unable to tell anyone even her name. Authorities were seeking passenger identities, the plane's origin, and destination. No aircraft was reported missing. No flight plan had been filed.

Pat's television blared to life with video of charred and twisted wreckage. A police officer, Sgt. Scott Morris, told an insistent reporter no further details were available. Pat could see the child's frightened face. She and Charlie hadn't had time for children. What might happen to that child now? The officer speculated the plane might have carried drugs. A "suspicious substance" had been found.

"Maybe I can help find out who she is!" Pat sprang

from her table. Half an hour later, she was in Mercy General's lobby.

"You don't understand. I found her after the crash!" In frustration, Pat was trying to pass an iron-jawed volunteer at the hospital's front desk. A family of six descended, distracting the volunteer. Pat backed away, tears stinging her eyes, and bumped into an immovable object.

"Nice to see you again." The voice, gruff with a hint of kindness, belonged to wide shoulders, a denim jacket, khaki pants, dark brown hair, brown eyes. He nodded to the desk volunteer, then offered Pat a quirky smile.

Flustered, she stammered, "Excuse me. Do I know you?"

"I could never forget a face like yours." He smiled again. Coming from him, it didn't sound like such a line.

"You're the officer from last night." Pat felt herself relax. "I'm trying to find her. Do you know where she is?"

"Third floor. Children's ward. I'm headed there myself." They fell in step toward the lobby elevators.

"Are you the officer I was reading about in the morning paper?"

"Misquoted." He frowned, but his eyes were

merry. "We're not supposed to mention drugs until the investigation's complete. Not much doubt about this one."

"Suppose they're all dead? Her whole family." A crazy, against-all-logic idea was forming in Pat's head. *She's alone. I'm alone. Why can't two people who find each other in the night . . .*

The elevator doors opened. Pat heard howling.

"That's her. I know it." She hurried down the hall, Scott Morris right behind her.

A nurse with a stethoscope hovered over the crib. The child was sitting up, rigid, red-faced, tears rolling from blue eyes. She saw Pat and stopped crying. The nurse turned. The child reached for Pat with chubby arms.

"Can I pick her up?"

"I don't think so," the nurse began, but the child's arms were tight around Pat's neck.

Scott Morris' quirky smile spread to a large grin.

"Hey, you've got a way with kids," he said admiringly. "You must have some of your own."

Pat blushed. That had been a touchy topic around her parents' dinner table.

"We'll find her next-of-kin. Just a matter of time," he predicted, unzipping a plastic tote. The brown teddy bear looked small in his large hands.

The child gave a squeal of joy. The bear disappeared into chubby arms.

"It's a miracle she's alive," the nurse offered, checking vital signs now that the child was occupied with the toy.

"That wasn't the only miracle last night." He said the words lightly. Pat blushed again. She had a crazy, against-all-logic thought.

Why can't two people who find each other in the night . . .

First Place Winner in NC Writers' Network West Flash Fiction contest, 2018.

Audacity and Nerve

The magazine's central office was quiet now. Obviously Norm Shallot, Pete Northan, Cindy Banks, and Jonathan Schmitt were elsewhere, probably huddled in plotting mode. Once again, Charisse Calcone had been shut out of their discussions and banned from the magazine's post-publication review.

"I'm in trouble," she surmised.

She waited behind the closed door in her small office cubicle, a windowless space, cold and functional. Shelves lined the facing wall, emptied hurriedly by the last occupant. Circle impressions marked the bottom shelf, residue of a green plant or two to brighten the drab room. Turnover at *Innuendo* was high, one of the reasons she had chosen to come to this particular publication.

She heard laughter and scattered footsteps down the hall. Shallot opened the door. He saw Charisse sitting quietly at her desk. He scowled and motioned her toward his office next door, the one with the pretentious gold lettered EDITOR on the panel. After ushering her in, he did not close the door. She heard shuffling and a giggle, as if others were within ear-shot. Co-conspirators, she suspected.

Shallot stood, putting his enormous desk between them. His tall, whip-thin shadow fell across the mahogany. He ran nervous fingers through dark hair slightly graying. He gave a hitch to pants around a middle barely thickening, an alpha slightly past his prime.

He pointed wordlessly to one of two armless chairs. He did not ask her to sit, but Charisse did, feeling like a child summoned to the school principal's office. In the give-me-no-backtalk voice Charisse had heard him use to underscore opinions he was sure no one would dare challenge, he began what sounded to her like a rehearsed speech.

"We're letting you go. There's duplication between your job and Cindy's. It's obvious to me we don't need two people performing the same functions."

There it was. No preamble. No thank you for good work but . . . Charisse had expected a showdown, even a stab in the back. But she had not foreseen this. She stared at him, forcing her voice not to waver when she answered.

"So you're firing me, even though I've only been here a month."

He shifted slightly, leaning over and resting his knuckles on the desk.

"No, not firing, exactly. Just call it streamlining." His smile was confident, imperious even. "It's been obvious to me from the beginning we wouldn't need two editorial assistants. That's not quite your title, but it's essentially the same position, now isn't it?"

He waited with a certain expectation for—what? For her to sob and fall to her knees in a plea, tearfully recounting how much she loved the work, or needed the money, begging him to reconsider, give her another chance? He seemed surprised, a trifle impatient, when she waited a couple of beats to respond.

"I see." She nodded, her gaze cool and unwavering. "And when do you expect me to leave?"

"Right now."

Charisse sat motionless for a moment, then got up from her chair. "All right. I'll get my things."

When she looked back at him, Shallot was smiling, staring toward the co-conspirators now coming through the door. He gave Cindy a wink.

"You have, of course, discussed this with Mr. Rupert?" Charisse threw the question casually over her shoulder. He stiffened.

"This is my department, and I run it as I see fit. I don't need to discuss personnel with Willard Rupert."

Now Charisse had her hand on the door. "Then I'll tell him. You know, of course, he hired me."

Shallot frowned. Pete, Cindy, and Jonathan, now all inside his office, froze and stared at her, perhaps reevaluating hastily formed opinions.

"No, I didn't know that. He didn't tell me. You just showed up with a memo saying you were to be put to work immediately."

"And you didn't ascertain the source of the memo?"

He shook his head. "No, I thought Personnel had sent it up along with you because somebody down there had the mistaken idea we needed extra help up here. They never check with me about much of anything."

A thunderous mask had replaced his self-satisfied smirk. His face flushed and he shuffled his feet, giving her a long look.

Charisse shrugged, returning her sweetest smile. "I think it only fair to tell you this. When he hired me, Mr. Rupert asked if I would assess the professionalism in this department. I will be sharing my opinions with Mr. Rupert. He's doing some reevaluation and planning to make some changes at *Innuendo*."

"He's out of town," Cindy squeaked from near the door. Her blonde curls bounced as she took a step backward. Pete shuffled his feet. Jonathan stared, eyes wide, mouth open.

"Oh, that won't matter." Charisse smiled at Cindy. "We're in touch."

Charisse returned to her cubbyhole office, slowly collected scarf, gloves, coat, and briefcase, and started down the hall, thinking how effective are the weapons of audacity and nerve when you have the chutzpah to use them. She recalled how she had employed such tactics to her advantage in the past. As she reached the hallway's end, Charisse heard pounding steps. Someone was running, hoping to stop her before the exit.

"Wait!"

She smiled in satisfaction. Audacity and nerve. Now a contrite Norm Shallot would ask her to stay. He would probably confide how he was having a very bad morning and had made a snap decision he obviously had not carefully considered. He might even offer an apology.

Pete, Jonathan, and Cindy would treat her differently too. The small office clique would fear she was indeed a spy sent to observe their performance. They would never mention her to Rupert, should they see him. Such a conversation with the magazine's mercurial publisher would be entirely too awkward.

Now she would stay if she liked or leave if she didn't, at a time of her own choosing. She would not tell them she had never met Willard Rupert.

Beauty in the Mundane

We all wait with anticipation for life's towering moments—sunsets that steal our breath, moonscapes that send shivers up our back, the laughter, the joy, the surprise announcement, the unexpected gift or promotion.

There is beauty in the mundane as well. Our day-to-day activities so often are viewed as drudgery, just tasks to complete, hours with minutes that drip so tediously we think an afternoon will never pass.

In truth, such moments compose much of our lives.

I am in the late autumn of my life, nearing the time of winter—the bleak midwinter, as Christina Rossetti so aptly put it. As I stand on the cusp of old age, I am making a conscious effort to practice patience in all things and find joy and beauty in the mundane.

I am working hard to set aside my ego, my plans for a busy day, or my concerns for an uncertain future so I can appreciate a winter morning when hills are enclosed in fog and distant mountains are capped with snow, or a summer evening when an unanticipated zephyr pushes away the heat of the day.

My roots plunge deeply into the ancient Blue Ridge Mountains and I am grateful for this. I believe all humankind seeks grounding to something so we do not see ourselves as mere dots on a blue sphere turning endlessly in an infinite universe.

The once-numerous family stock from which I rise is scattered to the four winds now. Families are smaller. Cousins are far away and hardly expected to stay in touch.

But my family's name is on the road where I lived, on the elementary school where children romp, in the community where I grew up and first retired. A mountaintop I could see from my front porch bears my grandmother's maiden name. There is great comfort in this.

Long after my lifespan, these guideposts will remain for future generations. They will know the names of my people, who passed this way.

Unanswered Prayers

"Please, God, let me die early."

I pray this prayer after spending time with my father. I watch him move slowly around the yard, occasionally stooping to pick up a small tree branch, an acorn, something else catching his eye.

He bends easily, I think. *He has difficulty straightening his spine but no trouble touching his toes. He is ninety-two. He does it better than I do!*

"Did you check the mail?" He asks the question without looking at me. He is wondering if the rural carrier has been on time.

"Hasn't come yet," I respond, practicing patience. This is the third time I have answered that question in the past half hour.

In his prime, my father was six feet tall, stubborn, and strong of will. He grew up on a Southern farm with three brothers and an independent-minded sister. She moved far away, but he spent most of his life on family land. He built his home a half mile from my grandfather's house.

He walked behind a plow, milked cows, pitched hay in summer heat. He left the land to serve in Patton's army, losing an eye in France when an enemy shell exploded on a building where he was sheltering, sending shrapnel flying. A proud veteran, he hardly mentions his vision loss, his military experience, his Purple Heart, or the grueling World War II days my generation can't even imagine.

Until recently, he planted a large garden, growing and harvesting beans, potatoes, corn, okra, cucumbers, and other vegetables my mother, a marvelous cook, prepared splendidly for the table. He no longer does that. He no longer drives a car or does many of the things he used to enjoy. Last week, he came into his house with skinned elbows. He has no idea what happened. He does not remember falling.

Sometimes he seems aware of his shortcomings, but we do not know whether he knows of his diagnosis. His mother had it—senile dementia, sometimes called sundowners. A brother developed Alzheimer's. His independent-minded sister, living alone, had it. A panicked daughter put her in a nursing home, against her will, after finding her forgetting to eat meals. She had lost thirty pounds.

Dementia is confounding and complicated. Dad carries on a brief conversation with me just as well as he might have three decades ago. He seems engaged, interested, and alert. He knows who he is. He knows who I am. We talk about the weather. But a quarter hour later, we may have the same conversation. And a quarter hour later, we may have it again.

"Did you check the mail?"

"No, Dad. Hasn't come yet."

I watch my father carefully, overwhelmed by my feelings of love, pity, anxiety for his future, and, selfishly, fear for my own. But my prayer was not answered. My grandmother, my dad, and my aunt all are gone now. So far, I do not have this family malady. Perhaps I am like my mother, who lived past 102.

Today, I am grateful when prayers sometimes go unanswered.

Contrasting Lives:
A Reflection on Friendship

I was digging in my flower garden when I found it, lying just beneath the soft rich soil. I don't know how it came to be there, but it dissolved my morning to tears and haunted the rest of my day. When I brushed away the dirt, the penny was new and shining, its burnished glow a mocking reminder of a promise not kept. On the coin, I saw not the face of President Lincoln but of Phyllis, looking at me with warm eyes that did not accuse but tugged at my soul nevertheless.

Like the copper coin, she was bright and sparkling in her life. My tears were drops of guilt, for Phyllis and for the vow I made as she lay dying. I have tried a dozen times in as many years to fulfill that vow, but the words would not come.

It was not a good year when I saw her last. I said goodbye to two great friends. She was one, Della the other. Phyllis taught me how to live, with verve and a joie de vivre unmatched by any other person I have ever known. Della showed me how to die, with dignity and grace and great strength, surrounded by friends bearing witness to her humanity and deep faith. Phyllis died with only her cousin, a nurse, nearby because everyone else feared to come near her. So many of Della's friends begged to say farewell, her family established visiting times at her bedside.

Phyllis and Della never knew each other. They had very little in common except milestones they shared: husbands who walked out, new second marriages, catastrophic illness, early death. And their friendship with me. I knew them at different places, different times. Yet I like to imagine how they might have touched each other had they met.

Phyllis was petite and blonde, with a pixie face not beautiful but utterly engaging. She was an energetic Southern California girl who married well and strutted her gifts in little theater productions. She never wanted or needed for much of anything except near the end, when, as she slipped away, she wanted desperately to be remembered.

Phyllis' husband, Tony, was a globe-trotting executive for a major oil company with responsibilities taking him to such exotic locales as Singapore and

Beijing. Sometimes Phyllis went along, but on extended trips, he generally left her alone at home to occupy herself with keeping a spotless house and tending a near-perfect body.

Phyllis loved diamonds, and he bought her many. She wore a two-carat pendant around her neck, a tear-shaped solitaire on her right pinkie, and a large emerald-cut gemstone above her wedding band. I saw her take them off only for aerobics classes.

She also had pedigreed dachshunds, which is how we met. My husband, Rob, and I advertised for a mate for our female, Shadow. Phyllis answered the ad. She and Tony brought over Trickster. While we forced small talk, the dogs did considerably more than get acquainted. They entangled beneath my dining room table and wouldn't come out. We were all childless city folk who treated our dogs like human offspring. When Shadow and Trickster didn't separate as quickly as we thought they should, we called the vet in panic. I can still hear his guffaws. After he caught his breath, he said that's what dogs were supposed to do, stop standing over them wringing our hands and they'd eventually come apart. They did, but our friendship didn't. When I held Phyllis' hand near the end, I reminded her of that and got a faint smile.

Della was tall, with wispy light brown hair she wore in a short pageboy style framing a strong face reflecting serious intent. She was big-boned with a natural grace and a crooked smile radiating an unexpected warmth. A studied weariness crossed her face from time to time. I thought it came from the burden of raising two children as a single mother.

Della never owned a dog or any other kind of pet. She poured every ounce of her energy into bringing up Neil and Rosalie, her teenagers. Rob and I, newcomers to the Atlanta suburbs, met her at church, where, standing among strangers, we felt like outcasts until a smiling woman crossed the room, hand outstretched, to introduce herself. Her Savannah-bred speech patterns reminded me of Spanish moss and lazy afternoons.

Della's enviable poise came from earning self-confidence the hard way, with little or no encouragement from a soulmate. I was to learn of that, and about her astonishing courage.

I joined the church choir, where Della was an outstanding member with a lilting soprano range that, with proper training, could have taken her to Broadway. My own rusty alto was hardly in her league.

Once Rob and I were fully settled in our new neighborhood, we threw a big party and invited some of our recent acquaintances. Della volunteered to bring the punch, concocted from her grandmother's special recipe. She crossed my threshold and tripped on my welcome mat. Della and two large jugs of raspberry liquid went flying in all directions. I helped her up, telling her I could sympathize because I was my family's klutz. We bonded right there. Afterward, we could double each other over with "punch" lines. People thought we were crazy.

When she wasn't fretting about her children or singing in the choir, Della spent working hours at the sheriff's department, where she was office manager and occasional dispatcher. She had plenty of stories to tell. Most of them she kept to herself. She had law enforcement's natural wariness of the press. After I told her I had been a crime reporter, I had to work hard to earn her trust. Eventually, she loosened, but she hardly ever wanted to discuss her work, or herself.

One year, just after Christmas, Della and I began rehearsals with a full orchestra for a presentation of Joseph Haydn's powerful "The Creation." On a soft night in early spring our large choir lifted an audience from its pews with the incomparable music. To this day, I consider my participation in that shared experience one of the soaring moments of my life.

While Della took the spotlight reluctantly, Phyllis loved to perform. She didn't have Della's gift, but she brought unbounded energy to choral parts in small community theater productions. The night she romped through *South Pacific*, she was the smallest member of the cast, but she commanded the stage nevertheless.

Phyllis and Tony loved to entertain. Sometimes they hosted dignitaries from Tony's oil excursions. I recall an entire Chinese delegation strolling through the backyard, where their Spanish-style home over-looked the sun-roasted Southern California coast. They owned a duplex on Manhattan Beach. When their renters moved, Phyllis told me we should look at the upstairs apartment. It was small for our needs, but the view was indescribable. The Pacific lapped practically in the front yard. She rented it to us on the spot for the same amount the previous couple had paid, a gesture infuriating Tony because he had intended to jack up the price.

It seemed to me Tony treated Phyllis rather harshly. He would criticize her unfairly and fuss if she wore something he considered "inappropriate." He hated media of all types and became obnoxious when he learned I had taken a job as a police reporter for the *Manhattan Beach Press*.

One hot summer day, Tony arrived at my door with a flinty glint in his brown eyes and a rehearsed speech at the ready.

"I have good news and bad news," he said triumphantly. "The bad news is I'm raising your rent. The good news is, I'm not going to raise it as much as I should."

"Then we'll be leaving," I snapped back. "We're thinking about going to the Olympic games, and we'll have to start saving now if we really want to."

As it happened, Rob's business called him South. We went not to the Olympics but to Atlanta. Six weeks later, I wept as Phyllis and I said goodbye.

The year I left Southern California was a bad time for her, she told me later. Her friend Marta moved to Oregon. She and Tony separated. She never volunteered the reason why, and I didn't pry. He took the dog. She kept the diamonds.

She visited us once after our move. Since I had known her, Phyllis had great legs, beautiful muscles in her arms, a tiny waist, and flat chest. Now she looked like Bernadette Peters. The implants were cold to touch and that bothered her, she said, but Tony had wanted her to get them. But soon after, they divorced, and she said she had a new boyfriend.

Shortly after Phyllis' visit ended and she returned to Southern California, Della's back began to ache. When her doctor finished his tests, the scans had revealed a large tumor. He sent her to University Hospital, where surgeons removed the growth and one kidney. Subsequent scans showed her cancer-free.

"It's the best present anybody could ever have," she announced at our choir Christmas party. Her faith and the support of her friends had pulled her through, she said.

Della had been a choir regular since I joined the church. Until her illness, she never missed a Sunday. The choir director, a handsome tenor who had studied with Atlanta's famous conductor Robert Shaw, finally summoned the courage to ask her out.

Even though Rob and I sent a card, we didn't hear from Phyllis that Christmas. This was unusual, and I fretted about it. My phone calls brought no response. Around midnight one cold January night, my telephone rang.

"I'm calling you from the hospital," she said without preamble in a voice small and unsteady. "I have AIDS and no T-cells left. Do you know what T-cells are?"

I told her I did.

"You must come to see me," she said. "Don't wait too long."

When I could rearrange my work schedule, I flew nonstop to California. I found her in a hospital in Newport Beach, in a room overlooking a spectacular view. The Pacific roared hard against the coastline. Sailboats shimmered on silken water. Her blue eyes burned in a white, defiant face. The implants looked like cantaloupes resting on her wasted body.

"Did I tell you I married Paul?" she said, recalling the boyfriend she had mentioned earlier. "I tried to eat some of my wedding cake, but I couldn't keep it down."

For three days, I stayed at her bedside as she volunteered what brought her to this room. After Tony left, she had found a replacement, but he turned into a one-night stand. His previous girlfriend had used drugs and was infected with the virus. She passed it to him. He gave it to Phyllis.

She didn't say much about the new husband. He never came to the hospital while I was there. Her mother and sisters hated him, she said. They thought he was after her diamonds and wouldn't be waiting long.

AIDS was a relatively new disease then, and many of the hospital staff were terrified of the symptoms, and of Phyllis. Her doctor looked at me with hooded eyes and stress lines on his face.

"You do know what's the matter with her, don't you?" he asked uncertainly.

Even in the hospital, Phyllis said people would call her in the middle of the night to whisper over the telephone. "You're going to die," they would hiss. "You've got AIDS. Why don't you die now?"

When she first learned of her disease, Phyllis had checked herself out of the hospital. On impulse, she took a plane to Hawaii, purchased $400 sunglasses, and headed to a craggy beach, watching the waves lap over lava rocks and listening to the surf singing in her ears. The reality seemed unbearable, the crushing weight of her illness and the glittering environment mocking her predicament.

After a few hours, she became deathly ill. As she lay on the sand, nausea washing over her and dizzy from dehydration, a handsome passerby stopped to offer assistance. Even in her illness, and quite helpless in her current state, Phyllis possessed a magnetism powerful enough to stop strangers in their steps. The man was a lonely tourist trying to reassemble his life after a wrenching divorce. He took Phyllis to his hotel, nursed her back to a functional state, and helped her to the airport. Her doctor returned her to the hospital immediately.

After we said goodbye, Phyllis' face hovered before me every moment of that long night flight back to Atlanta. I have tried to imagine her since, but she never becomes real to me. In one more midnight phone call, she gasped in a frantic voice that she was coming to see me.

"Honey, you can't go to Atlanta," I heard a woman whisper in the background, adding a hushed coda. "You can't go anywhere."

Her sister telephoned a few weeks later to tell me Phyllis had died at home with her cousin, the nurse in attendance. The family scattered her ashes over the Pacific.

After I heard the news of Phyllis' passing, I felt numb, empty, and incredibly sad. I could not fathom the stilling of that boundless energy. Try as I might, I still cannot conjure her as I last saw her.

Instead, I see her on my breezeway, holding a squirming puppy in each arm. She has come from the beach. Her skin is the color of honey, her curls ruffled by the wind. She is laughing, a delighted tinkling sound. She has just told me how, in payment for the mating of our dogs and the resulting pups, she will take the runt of the litter. He nuzzles her face, licks her nose, nestles against her warmth, and goes to sleep.

Word of Phyllis' death came in early summer, just as Della's cancer recurred, this time in her spine. They would treat it with an experimental drug, doctors told her. She would not surrender, she vowed. Her daughter was about to depart for college. Her son had just earned a spot on his high school football team. She was seriously dating the choir director, who was divorced with children of his own.

Mindful of her condition and a future in jeopardy, they rushed a wedding. The congregation packed the church to watch two families blend. Everyone said never was a bride more beautiful. Her new husband was a great gift so she would not have to face her doubtful future alone, she told them at the reception.

"You're the bravest person I've ever met," I said to her new mate.

"I don't know about that," he whispered with a glance toward his bride.

After a short honeymoon, they took a cruise with close friends to the Bahamas. Aboard ship, pain returned in Della's back.

"We knew it would be fast," her husband told concerned friends who dropped by with gifts and food.

In the hospital, doctors suppressed her immune system, hoping for positive impact from the latest treatments. I donned sterile garb and gloves to avoid carrying extra germs into her room. Despite her advancing illness, she smiled at me and seemed the same. As I was leaving, her mother thanked me for stopping by.

"You'd be surprised how many people don't come," she said. "I just don't think they can face it."

As Della's illness began to steal her breath and doctors could do no more to halt the march of her disease, they sent her home with oxygen tanks and powerful painkillers. Her family moved her bed downstairs so she could prop up on pillows and receive visitors. The constant stream of friends forced her family to set visiting hours.

When I last saw her, we sat quietly, holding hands without speaking. Her fine bones glowed through pale skin. She squeezed my hand and went to sleep. Three days later, she was gone. Her family buried her in her wedding dress.

Today, in my memory, I often ponder how Della and Phyllis might have touched each other, had they become friends. Had she known Phyllis well, Della might have breached the walls of their differing personalities. Perhaps she could have cracked the thin veneer of perfection Phyllis tried to wear. Maybe Phyllis could have convinced Della life was not quite so serious, that abandoning decorum for spontaneous laughter was acceptable from time to time.

They might have connected in such a way that Della could have shared with Phyllis the source of her own great strength. Perhaps she could have helped Phyllis rise above the terrible loneliness that forced her into the arms of a stranger and led her to contract the disease ultimately stripping away her life.

I sat with both of my friends near their deaths, but those shadows are fading. Instead, I see them both full of strength and joy. Phyllis is in the California sun, laughing, with an armful of squirming puppies. Della is singing in the choir, her powerful voice rising above the music.

As I work in the soft soil where I found the penny, I remember what my friends have taught me: Life is a garden. If left untended, weeds will intrude and overrun it. Yet the garden can be a verdant expression of the very best life can offer, no matter how briefly it flourishes and blooms.

Della's last words to me were, "I love you, too."

Phyllis' last words were, "Write about me sometime." I have kept my promise, but I'm not sure this is what she had in mind.

On a recent morning as I walked in my garden, with fog wrapping the distant hills in a glove of gray, I said goodbye to my friends again, thanked them for their smiles, their tears, and what they taught me.

I remember them well, I think of them often, and I will not forget.

More Than Pumpkins

Ruby Corrine Darby applied the candy-apple red very carefully, outlining her lips so they appeared fuller. She brushed her long brown hair, thankful for naturally blonde highlights, and swept it back from her face, highlighting her cheekbones. Stepping into the dress, she was careful not to wrinkle it. She wore no underwear. Her high-heeled black pumps went into a shopping bag. She didn't want her sister Delta or Aunt Nona to see them.

Facing the long mirror, she surveyed her image. The jungle-print frock was shorter than she usually wore, her long legs appearing attached to her waist. The dress's ruffled top, plunging in a low V to reveal her cleavage, made her small breasts seem larger. The dress worked.

She gave a deep sigh and pulled on her gray raincoat. This fresh October morning was cloudy, carrying the strong promise of a later cloudburst.

The weather was fortunate. A raincoat, too, would hide her intentions. So would the black flats she pulled on her feet. She pressed her palms to her face. *I must not think of what I'm about to do. I must not think at all. I must just do.*

Hearing the angry horn, she drew back the curtain as Daryl's white pickup pulled into the driveway. Straightening the raincoat, she squared her shoulders, preparing to face the morning's first test.

"Why you wearin' so much makeup for jus' a trip to the grocery store?" Her sister tossed her a pointed look. "And ain't you gonna be too hot in that raincoat?"

"Just felt like red lipstick today." Corrine brushed a lock of hair from her cheek and gave her younger sister a tentative smile. "I didn't want to carry this coat. Easier to just wear it. Be rainin' soon."

Aunt Nona was in the kitchen giving Roger his breakfast. He sat hunched in his wheelchair and didn't look up. He simply stared at some fixed point in space, at a place only he could see. In his chair, he seemed more boy than man.

Twins Jenny and Jonus had already caught their school bus. Two-year-old Ricky was babbling from his highchair, waving his small hands happily in the air. Delta gave him a spoonful of cereal with milk.

"You gon' be long?" Delta cast a rueful glance in

Corrine's direction while wiping milk dribbling from Ricky's chin. "I got some things to do today m'self."

"Don't know for sure," Corrine replied without looking at her. "I'm going with Daryl and he's already mad for making him wait. We might make some stops later."

"Well, don' be late," Delta's parting words followed Corrine out the door toward their brother's old truck. *I'm quite certain we'll be late*, Corrine responded silently. *The trade always gets better with the dark.*

***

The truck stop had been especially fruitful a few weeks ago. After five hours, she came home with $325. A return engagement was not in the cards, however. The Singleton sisters made it pointedly clear this was their turf. Shaking their fists in her face, they told her to get lost.

This time, she and Daryl made for the rest stop on Interstate 26 between Orangeburg and Savannah. The back of his pickup was loaded with pumpkins, orange, ripe, and ready for Halloween.

Daryl parked his vehicle in the far corner of the rest stop, angling it so the truck bed advertised its orange wares. The pumpkins would catch the eye of motorists when they wheeled in for relief from the road. What they saw next would be Corrine, tottering in her black pumps, standing just outside the passenger side's open door, raincoat discarded, skirt hiked to the top of her bare thighs, one leg angled outward in invitation, the other resting on the truck's rocker panel, her hand lazily moving to and from the cigarette between her parted lips.

If this stance didn't work, she would take a come-hither walk through the parking lot, up to the restrooms if necessary, meeting each man with a direct stare and a smile. Sometimes they just looked away. Once, a tall, serious chap gave her a verbal dressing down. She suspected he might be a preacher.

The buyers would be invited to the back seat of Daryl's truck while he went for a stroll and smoke. The truckers welcomed her into the cab of their big rigs. Often, they had sleeping compartments behind the cab.

Today's first customer, a stringy blond guy in his mid-twenties, rasped, "How much?" When she told him, he nodded, and she hustled him into the pickup and closed the door. As they began to move in tandem, she took her usual mind trip far away.

***

It was a Friday night at the Mile High Tavern, a few miles down the road from the three-bedroom bungalow they shared with Aunt Nona. After their parents died, Nona, who had never married and claimed no other family than the sister she had lost, promised to care for the two girls in return for company and domestic help. She had a healthy pension from years with the long-defunct phone system, but some around-home chores were getting too much for her aging bones. Their older brother Daryl already had his own place, just a shack really, attached to a couple of acres he was trying to farm. Daryl worked a series of odd jobs, growing a little produce to sell, but he was making ends meet. The sisters, however, were still in high school.

Corrine didn't mind helping her aunt, who was eternally cheerful, not demanding in the least. She treated the girls, seventeen and fifteen at the time, as grown-ups. Best of all, she never gave them quizzical looks when they came home late or confronted them with third-degree questions.

"Life's too short," she would say. "If you never make any mistakes, how can you learn anything? Just don't get into trouble you can't get out of."

The days became predictable. The teens went faithfully to school and graduated. They looked for jobs around the local area, but opportunities were few. Delta babysat regularly for Mrs. Cates, a neighbor who held a job at a local cafe. Corrine cashiered at a mid-sized market, usually on the night shift.

When they were of legal age and had a few days off, they liked to spend evenings at the Mile High. The tavern's name was a standing joke, referring to the free flow of drugs rather than the altitude. The jukebox was loud, the beer watery and cheap. Corrine and Delta knew most of the customers, but Calhoun County's dating pool was limited. The girls had been out with most of the regulars at some point. Nothing seemed to bloom into a lasting relationship.

They did not know the tall man who came one Friday night wearing his US Army uniform, staring at them with blue-eyed fascination and a gap-toothed grin.

"Haven't seen you around here before," said Corrine, who was more outspoken than Delta.

"Been around. Home on leave. Mind if I sit?" He pulled up a bar stool.

So it began. When Roger Darby asked her out, Corrine hesitated. He seemed so much older, in manner if not age. He was twenty-seven, on his own for a long time, he said. He had joined the army when he came of age. He liked her, he said, because she wasn't one of the too-shy maidens or overly pretentious teasers he usually met.

***

The morning's second customer was a fat grinning man in his mid-fifties, smelling of too much beer and old sweat. He wanted to talk, to ask her name, where she was from. She gave him vague responses until he offered her a fifty-dollar bill. When they climbed into Daryl's truck, he wanted to play nasty, but Corrine set him straight in a hurry.

"Then I want my money back. Right now." His broad face transformed from leer to snarl.

"With pleasure," Corrine snapped. "With me, it's straight or no go. I'm worth it, but I don't do the rough stuff." She thrust the crumpled bill into his dirty fingers.

He gave her a long, thoughtful look, nodded silently, and sheepishly handed the money back. Soon Corrine forgot about the sweating, grunting man and began again to revisit her past . . .

***

When she had told Roger, home on his second leave, that she was definitely pregnant and they were going to have twins, no less, he grinned with gap-toothed delight and suggested they get married in a hurry. And they did.

Jenny and Jonus were born nine months later, looking like two different peas from the same pod. Roger said he was the happiest man on earth to have a daughter and a son. But then he disclosed his new orders: leaving soon for Afghanistan. He would be gone for several months. He promised to send money to her and the twins every payday.

Corrine and the babies continued to live with Nona and Delta in the bungalow. Delta was happy to help care for her niece and nephew, and Nona was delighted to watch the rambunctious twins develop and grow. Delta freed Corrine to take on enough work at the market so that she moved to day shift. Soon, she was promoted to assistant store manager.

Roger's letters and checks arrived like clockwork, as promised. The babies were changing every day. When Corrine came home at night, sometimes too weary to lift them in her arms, she felt pangs of jealousy. Jenny, especially, reached for Delta more than anyone else.

One afternoon, Corrine got a message from Roger. He would be home for Christmas. Giddy with anticipation, the sisters transformed the small house with twinkling lights, wreaths, garlands, and pinecones they sprayed with gold paint. The twins stared in fascination at the spectacle and set about undecorating the Christmas tree. In exasperation, Corrine and Delta maneuvered the large fir to the front porch and installed a small pine on a table out of reach of tiny fingers.

Roger's leave flew by in a too-short breath. The twins cooed with glee as their daddy morphed into a horsey they could ride and offered long legs they could climb. When he departed, he left them crying and Corrine pregnant.

"Don't worry, honey," he promised. "This will be my last tour. Soon I'll be home, and we'll get our own place. I'll find a good job and take care of our family."

Ricky was born eight months later, a long, complicated labor putting both mother and child at risk. A stern-faced doctor told Corrine there would be no more children. He had removed her ovaries and uterus to stop the bleeding. Her recovery would take patience.

Nona sent a message to Roger, telling him he had

a second son. When she felt stronger, Corrine wrote a long letter detailing the doctor's comments.

Roger seemed thrilled with his new son, upset she was facing recovery alone, sorry he could not be there to help. Six months and it would all be over, he said. His duty stint was ending, and he would be home to stay.

***

Daryl had a couple of buyers for his pumpkins. They wanted to surround the truck bed for a thorough inspection. Corrine took a detour to a row of parked big rigs near a large stand of pines. A sleepy driver lowered his window and asked if she was interested in a "two-fer." Not sure what he meant, Corrine hesitated until a second head, grinning, popped out of the window. She nodded and climbed into the cab. The two, younger than she was, required an hour before satisfaction, but at the end, she left them so happy they gave her a $100 bill.

When she returned to Daryl and his truck, she found the bed half empty.

"You had a good customer or two or three," she observed. He pulled his dirty tee over a stomach so round it looked like one of his pumpkins and nodded.

"You, too, looks like." He gave her wrinkled dress a once-over.

"I'm done for the day and look what I got. Want some supper?" She waved the bill at him.

He cast another disapproving glance over her rumpled appearance and disheveled hair and gave a small shrug. "You're not goin' like that."

"I'll pull on my raincoat." She smirked. "Let's go find a burger. I'm hungry."

Sitting in the back booth at the local hamburger joint, she endured her brother's glower.

"How long you gonna keep doing that stuff? It ain't right."

"I know, but we need the money. We gotta eat. There's the kids, always hungry."

"Too bad you quit your job at the market. I thought you was doin' real good."

"Yeah, Willy Klontz thought I was doin' real good. I was, too, until I couldn't stand his pawing anymore."

Daryl's remarks and his frowning glances brought a rush of black memories, all the way back to the day her life transformed.

As she watched her brother chow down on a double cheeseburger and a plate of fries, Corrine lost her appetite and began to pick at her burger.

She had been home from the hospital with newborn Ricky for about a month when two men in uniform knocked on the front door. Nona answered and called to her with a trembling voice. Corrine, still spending most days in bed, pulled on a thin robe and padded to the living room.

"Ma'am, we're sorry to come here to tell you this," one of the uniforms began. But she knew. Something awful had happened to Roger.

"He's dead, isn't he?" She heard her own trembling voice, her body swaying. The room began to spin.

"Oh, no, ma'am." The other uniform stepped forward to steady her. "He's not dead at all. But there was an accident, and we understand he's badly hurt. Why don't you sit down, and we'll tell you what we know."

Roger was riding in an armored vehicle when a land mine exploded beneath it. Three people died, but he survived and was in hospital care. He would be there for a long while, they told her. His back was fractured. There was an issue of nerve damage in his legs. No, they did not know when he would come home, but she could fly to see him, at government expense, if she desired.

When Corrine's head cleared and she stopped

shaking, reason returned. She told them about her newborn needing round-the-clock care. She was still too weak to make such a journey. She would wait for Roger here at home.

Five months of recuperation and rehabilitation restored Roger to an upright position, but he would never regain the use of his legs. When she and Delta met him at the Atlanta airport, Corrine hardly recognized the gaunt, shrunken specter who was wheeled out to them. Seeing his body broken beyond repair was one thing. His refusal to meet her eyes was another.

"I'm sorry, honey," he whispered. "I'm so sorry. I didn't plan on this."

The twins stared at the stranger in the wheelchair. Jonas became withdrawn in his daddy's presence. Jenny gave Roger a long look and returned to her dolls. Roger seemed to take little interest in baby Ricky. Day by day, he retreated further until he hardly spoke at all. Corrine and Nona scoured the county for help, from the local Veterans Administration office and the Department of Social Services to the county welfare office.

Eventually, a home healthcare aide began to come three times weekly to help with Roger's care. A nurse appeared weekday mornings to help clean his tubes, bathe him, and tend to other medical needs. A psychiatric social worker from the VA sat down for a lengthy conference with Nona and Corrine.

"He has a severe case of PTSD. Do you know what that is? Post-traumatic stress disorder is treatable, but it's going to require his getting some help."

With the aid of a VA contact and a sympathetic auto dealer where Daryl did freelance mechanical work, Nona was able to purchase a used SUV and equip it to accommodate Roger's wheelchair. Then began arduous treks to the VA center in Columbia, where Roger was assigned a psychiatric workup and a series of counseling sessions.

Corrine knew very little about PTSD. She was told to avoid pressuring Roger into talking about his war experience. That was hardly an issue since Roger rarely spoke at all. It seemed he had hardly looked at her since his return from Afghanistan. Don't take his behavior personally, she was told.

Roger was sent home with medication, but Corrine saw no improvement. The pills made him sleepy. Almost every time she passed his chair, he was dozing. At times, she felt she had no husband at all. To her, he seemed a stranger. The mischievous blue eyes and gap-toothed grin that had drawn her to him long had faded.

As a result, she spent more and more time at the market. As assistant manager, she supervised a staff of frequently transient cashiers, grocery baggers, and stockroom boys. Few of the employees remained longer than six to eight months. Frequently, she filled in at checkout or helped stock shelves and take inventory. Under the watchful eye of the market's bookkeeper, she took a turn helping there too.

Late one night, when she stayed to help organize the stockroom, she heard footsteps. Turning, she came face to face with Willy Klontz, the market's owner and manager. Willy, middle-aged and paunchy, was a tough boss but ultimately fair. About five foot ten with thinning brown hair and brown eyes encased in thick glasses, he ran his market like the drill sergeant he once was, peppering cashiers with questions, suggestions, and directions. At first, he intimidated Corrine, but as she took on more responsibility and did her job to his satisfaction, she came to respect him.

She thought the feeling was mutual.

"You've been doing a good job, Corrine," he said, stepping into the stockroom and watching her align cans of beans and peas. "I'm considering taking a little vacation, and I'm thinking of leaving you in charge, if you think you can handle it."

Surprised and pleased, she turned to face him. "I appreciate you asking me. I'll do my best."

He stepped a little closer. "I know you have a lot going on at home, a lot of responsibilities. Actually, I don't know how you do it."

"I have good help. Aunt Nona helps with Roger. We have health workers almost every day too. Delta takes Ricky with her when she babysits, and Mrs. Cates doesn't mind. Her kids like to play with him."

"It must be hard for you, though, your husband and all."

She shrugged. "Well, I'm managing the best I can."

"I'm sure you are. But it still must be difficult, an attractive woman like yourself, with no man to—"

He was standing in her personal space. He reached out a plump hand and brushed a strand of hair from her face. Corrine didn't move.

"I just want you to know that if you ever want or need anything . . . I'm here. You've got an admirer."

He was so close she could feel his breath. It smelled of mints or mouthwash. Corrine remained motionless, barely breathing.

He dropped his hand and stepped back. She exhaled softly. He started for the door, giving her a small smile.

"Just remember what I said. I'll let you know if I can get this vacation nailed down."

Mute, she nodded as he closed the door. Corrine reached for the stock shelf to steady her shaking knees. A month later, Corrine was in the stockroom again when Willy entered. His steps seemed to have purpose.

"Vacation plans?" She was arranging sacks of flour and meal.

He didn't answer her. She felt his hands on her shoulders, his body pushing against her back.

"Mr. Klontz, please . . ." She tried to move, but his grip was firm.

"Come on, Corrine. You know you want to. You're a strong, healthy woman, and you need it. And God knows, I do—"

Summoning all her strength, she tried to push him away, but he was strong, forcing her back, back against stacks of flour, down on pads of packing blankets. The encounter didn't last very long, and later, when she tried to recall just how it had happened, she was not able to. She only knew she was sitting on the sacks, sobbing, and he was standing over her, zipping his pants.

"If you say a word about this to anyone—anyone, you hear—it will be your word against mine. I will deny it, and I will fire you. Is that understood?"

He left her alone without another word.

Days following became a cat-and-mouse game. She took every opportunity to avoid being near him. He took every opportunity to lean over her shoulder at the checkout line, to brush against her on the produce aisles.

One afternoon, he told her vacation plans were arranged and he wanted to brief her on what she would need to know in his absence. Reluctantly, she followed him into his office and watched as he shut the door.

He stuck strictly to business at first. She would come in early and leave late, see the aisles were well-stocked, keep a watchful eye on stock boy Bruce Lemont, whom he suspected was stealing, and tally receipts at day's end.

Corrine nodded, forcing herself to meet his eyes.

"Well, that's about it. I'm sure you can do this, or I wouldn't be leaving the store in your hands."

"How long will you be away?"

"Just four or five days. I haven't taken the wife to the mountains in a long while. We're just going to Gatlinburg. You can reach me if you need anything."

"I'll call you if we have any problems." She stood up and gave him a small smile.

"Corrine, there is one more thing." He came swiftly around the desk and put his hands on her shoulders. She felt herself flinch, but she steeled herself not to move away.

"You must know how I feel about you. I'll do anything for another—" He stopped.

She shook her head.

"I can't. You know about Roger and the kids. I just can't."

He looked thoughtful for a second. "I know you need the money, so I have a proposition for you." He reached in his back pocket and took a $100 bill from his wallet.

"It's yours if you will. Just this once."

She took the money, hating herself. Afterward, as she straightened her clothing, he closed the door with a smirk.

The next day in the market, she felt his protracted gaze, but she could not look at him. The day after, he began his vacation.

Corrine told no one. She lay in bed listening to Roger's ragged breathing, recalling what easy money it had been, how much they had needed it, how it hadn't lasted long, and at the end how she had something for it, something they could use.

But I don't think I can do it with him again, she told herself. *Anybody but him.*

Corrine kept the market running during Klontz's vacation. He thanked her profusely when he returned and gave her a suggestive look, raising his eyebrows. Then she knew. The next day, she pushed a letter of resignation under his office door and left the market for good.

After that, Corrine haunted truck and rest stops. At first, she made little progress, and she hated herself for what she was doing. She also ran afoul of the Singleton sisters and other women who prowled truck stops and had staked out territories. Truckers derisively called them "lot lizards."

After a time, she became discouraged and applied for unemployment. That office turned her down because she had left a paying job abruptly. She suspected Klontz had given them an earful about how unappreciative she was.

Delta and Nona were mystified at Corrine leaving her market job. She was fired because business was slow, and Klontz was cutting staff, she told them. When they asked why he chose her, she devised various scenarios. When she vanished for hours from the bungalow, she said she was looking for work. Only Roger suspected. One afternoon, as she was putting on makeup and combing her hair, he looked at her with probing eyes.

"I know what you're doing, Corrine," he said. It was the first words he had spoken to her in months. She whirled, ready with a dozen explanations, but he just turned his head away. Daryl, too, figured it out in a hurry.

"I heard something about you," he told her after stopping by with a sack of fresh tomatoes. "I didn't believe it at first, but now I think it's true. Is it?"

"It is what it is," she said, not raising her eyes from chopping cabbage for slaw. "We gotta eat."

"You'd think you could have found something better to do with yourself." He scowled.

Angry, she whirled on him. "You find me a decent-paying job, where I can make forty to fifty and sometimes even a hundred dollars an hour, and I'll quit. I have to have money to take care of these kids. Jonus and Jenny needed new shoes, and book bags for school, and I got them."

He shrugged. "Well, I'll help you if you want to quit and try to find somethin' decent."

"Like what?"

"I dunno, but I'll look around. I finally found a gig for myself I think might turn into more than part-time."

"What's that?"

"You know I been workin' down at George's mechanic shop for about a year on weekends and days when he's real busy. He says business is pickin' up and he might start usin' me full-time." Her brother, shaggy hair protruding from under his baseball cap, scruffy beard badly needing a trim, T-shirt streaked with sweat and oil, frankly looked as if he already worked as a mechanic and had just come from the job.

"And when does he think that might be?"

"Right after first of the year," Daryl said. "Meantime, I'll just keep workin' weekends and whenever he calls me in to help."

He gave her a sharp look, changing the subject.

"That stuff you're doin' can be dangerous, Corrine. Maybe I oughta keep an eye on you when I can. Take you to the truck stops an' . . ."

She shrugged. "Nothing bad's happened yet. If you want, you can. I'll just keep on keepin' on for a while."

He sighed and stood up.

"I got me a pretty good crop comin' in on the two

acres. Nice stand of beans, and they'll be pumpkins aplenty for fall."

***

So, Daryl brought his bumper pumpkin crop first to the truck stop, then to the rest stop, and finally parked the truck just outside the local hamburger diner while he and Corrine ate their evening meal. Already two people had come to the counter to ask whether those pumpkins outside were for sale.

Grinning happily, Daryl was handling his third transaction when Corrine's cell phone jangled in her raincoat pocket.

"Corrine, is that you? Please come home. I need you." It was Nona's voice, laced with panic.

"What's wrong, Auntie?"

"It's Roger. He's had some sort of a seizure. The paramedics are here. I think they're taking him to emergency."

Hurriedly, Corrine paid the bill. In the hospital's emergency room, they found Nona, white-faced and frightened, talking to the admitting nurse.

"I'm his wife. Can I see him?" Corrine recognized the nurse, who shopped occasionally at the market. She buzzed Corrine through interlocking doors.

Roger lay in a cubicle, surrounded by nurses, technicians, and the ER doctor.

"He's had a serious seizure," the doctor told Corrine. "He quit breathing for a time, and we thought we'd lost him. We've intubated him and he'll be on a respirator. I've made arrangements to transfer him to the ICU."

"Can I see him?" Corrine asked tentatively.

"Yes, but he won't be able to respond to you," the doctor said. "He's unconscious and we don't know how long he might remain that way."

So began a vigil that took all their strength. Seven hours later, Corrine was able to go home, remove her too-hot raincoat, take a shower, and get some sleep. Roger spent the next six days in intensive care while Corrine, Delta, Daryl, and Nona juggled near-sleepless hospital nights with demanding days caring for the twins and Ricky at home.

Roger's condition remained unchanged. When he showed very little response, the doctor had him transferred to the Veterans Administration hospital in Columbia. He died there three days later, without having said a word, without opening his eyes, without saying goodbye. Corrine was numb.

"I know I did wrong, I did him wrong," she

sobbed on Daryl's shoulder before the funeral. "But what could I do?"

Roger was buried in his military uniform in the local interfaith cemetery with full military honors arranged by people from the Veterans Administration office. The twins watched wide-eyed, covering their ears as rifles fired in salute. Corrine held Ricky in her arms. Wrenching back tears, she accepted the folded stars and stripes. Afterward, Corrine, Delta, and Nona took the children home, fed them, rocked Ricky, and tucked them all into bed. Emotionally spent, Corrine sat on the front porch steps with a glass of cool water, staring at a sickle moon in the October night. She talked to Roger, hoping he could hear her.

"Roger, I'm so sorry. I made some terrible choices, but I didn't know what else to do," she sobbed. "I couldn't talk to Aunt Nona, or Delta. They would have been so disappointed in me. I couldn't talk to you. You couldn't hear me. I've been lost, and so alone."

The hour was very late. Corrine stiffened. Headlights were climbing the driveway. She brushed her cheeks with the backs of her hands and sighed with relief when she saw Daryl's old truck. He climbed out and joined her on the steps.

"How you doin' really?" He slid an arm around her shoulder. She leaned her head against his warmth.

"Oh, Daryl. I feel so confused. I know I've been on such a bad trip. I just didn't know what else to do." Her shoulders shook. "I want to get off this thing I've been doing. I want to honor Roger somehow, to honor his memory, by never turning another trick, never doing that again. Ever."

"You mean that?" Daryl faced her in the moonlight.

"More than anything. I don't want to do it anymore."

"I think I know somethin'. Let me look into it a little."

"What?"

"Can't say for sure. I just need to talk to somebody."

"About me?"

"Yep. I been thinkin' about this a little. I got an idea." He replaced his arm around her, giving her a brotherly hug. "Don't worry, Sis. You oughta get to bed. You look awful, y'know."

Corrine felt herself smile. Her big brother always had a talent for forcing a change of mood from his kid sister. She kissed his bristly cheek.

"Yeah, and you need a shave, y'know?"

Daryl was back in a couple of days.

"I talked to George down at the car shop. I told you he was gonna hire me full-time after Christmas. He needs a part-time bookkeeper, too. Didn't you keep some books at that market?"

"I did a little, not much." Corrine was juggling Ricky on her lap. The chubby toddler reached for his uncle. Daryl laughed and took him in his arms.

"Then you oughta go an' talk to him. I think he could use some help. You could take some classes down at that community college, too. That's where I learned how to be a mechanic."

"You don't think he knows about—" She dropped her gaze.

Daryl shrugged. "Maybe he does and maybe he don't. Maybe it won't matter."

He took a long look at his sister. She seemed distraught.

"I think I might know somewhere else you can get some help, some *real* help, if you really mean you want to turn your life around."

Corrine stiffened. "Oh yeah? And where's that?"

"I've been going to the Maranatha Church down the road. I can't explain it, but I think I found somethin' there."

Corrine stared at him. "And just what is it you've found exactly?"

"Why don't you come with me and see for yourself?" he said.

This story is entirely fiction, but the idea was based on fact.

My husband and I were traveling south on I-26, looking for some saw grass and Spanish moss relaxation. Just past the Orangeburg, South Carolina exit, a white extended-cab pickup truck whizzed by us on the freeway. The truck bed was loaded with pumpkins—big, orange, ripe, round indicators of Halloween fast approaching.

I remarked to my husband, "There goes a farmer with his fall crop, heading for a market in Savannah or Charleston. Look at those pumpkins!"

A dozen miles later, we pulled into a freeway rest stop. Before us, moving slowly through the parking lot was the pumpkin-packed pickup. The disheveled driver wheeled into a parking space across from us, emerging wearing a gray sweat-stained T-shirt that struggled to cover a girth so rotund it was reminiscent of the pumpkins.

What stunned us, however, emerged from the passenger side. She was mid-thirties, brownish-blond hair in a ponytail. She wore a dress with some type of jungle print, so short and low-cut it barely covered the essentials, bottom and top. Most striking were the ridiculous black pumps on which she proceeded to stalk the rough pavement of the parking lot.

His intention might have been to sell pumpkins. If any doubts remained about hers, they vanished when she struck a pose, one leg angled outward, an arm draped loosely on the open truck door while she casually smoked a cigarette and eyed the male passersby with a probing and calculating appraisal.

We returned to the freeway. Soon, the pickup passed us again and headed off the ramp toward Savannah. Then my husband observed how people are driven to strange and desperate actions when they are in dire economic straits.

I began to think about that. What might force a woman into such a situation? And who were they? A starving couple? A pimp and his prostitute?

Hence, this story. The main character is, of course, based on the Mel Tillis song recorded by Kenny Rogers & The First Edition, "Ruby, Don't Take Your Love to Town."

About the Author

Lorraine Martin Bennett is a print, web, and broadcast journalist who grew up in the rural Martins Creek Community near Murphy, North Carolina, graduated with her high school class journalism medal, and received a scholarship to UNC Chapel Hill, where she earned her degree. Her career began on the *Atlanta Journal*, where she wrote features, covered news, and met her late husband, Tom, also a journalist. She was hired by the *Los Angeles Times* and became the newspaper's first woman to head a domestic bureau.

She joined Ted Turner's fledgling CNN as a news writer, becoming copyeditor, producer, and editorial manager before ending her television career at CNN International.

In retirement, she writes essays, short stories, flash fiction, and poetry, and still practices her craft by copyediting and occasionally writing for the *Clay County Progress.*

Her essays have appeared in the Personal Story Publishing Project (Daniel Boone Footsteps, Winston-Salem), and her poetry has been published by the Huntsville Literary Association. Her first novel, a psychological thriller titled *Cat on a Black Moon*, was published by Austin Macauley (London, Cambridge, New York) in 2023. A sequel, *Darla*, was published by the same group in 2024, and a third novel, *20 Seconds to Midnight*, is due for publication in 2025.

Other Books by
LORRAINE MARTIN BENNETT

Cat on a Black Moon
Darla
20 Seconds to Midnight